I'm a Little Teapot

I'm a little teapot, short and stout,

Here is my handle, here is my spout,

When I get all steamed up hear me shout,

Tip me over and pour me out.

Baa Baa Black Sheep

Baa, baa, black sheep,

Have you any wool?

Yes, sir, yes, sir,

Three bags full.

One for the master,

One for the dame,

And one for the little boy

Who lives down the lane.

Miss Polly Had a Dolly

Miss Polly had a dolly

Who was sick, sick, sick,

So she called for the doctor

To be quick, quick, quick;

The doctor came

With his bag and his hat,

And he knocked at the door

 With a rat-a-tat-tat.

He looked at the dolly

And he shook his head,

And he said "Miss Polly,

Put her straight to bed."

He wrote out a paper

For a pill, pill, pill,

"I'll be back in the morning

With the bill, bill, bill."